The Attic Toys

OXFAM
THE UNLOVED BEAR

FREE STAND-UP TOY

This is the Property of some sort of Oxfam Esq.

D0281991

MARGARET STUART BARRY

PICTURES BY TESSA RICHARDSON-JONES

for
Alex and Sophie

The attic toys

OXFAM
THE UNLOVED BEAR

MARGARET STUART BARRY
Pictures by Tessa Richardson-Jones

First published in Great Britain in 1995.
Text copyright © 1995 Margaret Stuart Barry.
Illustrations © 1995 Tessa Richardson-Jones.
The moral right of the author has been asserted.

Bloomsbury Publishing PLC, 2 Soho Square, London W1V 6HB.
A CIP catalogue record for this book is available from The British Library
ISBN 0 7475 2230 8 pb
ISBN 0 7475 2263 4 hb
Text design by AB3.
Printed and bound in Great Britain
by William Clowes (Beccles) Ltd,
Beccles and London.

• CONTENTS •

CHAPTER ONE

A New Arrival

EVERYONE in the big attic was excited: a new toy was coming to stay. "I'll fetch him," cried Puff Puff, the little train. He rattled off across the attic floor and onto the landing, whistling loudly.

At the other end of the landing was a steep flight of stairs which went down to ...somewhere or other. All the toys had come up this staircase from Somewhere.

Puff Puff waited expectantly for the new arrival. He had overheard it was going to be a bear of some sort. He hoped it would be golden brown and very fluffy.

The new arrival was a very long time in

coming, so Puff Puff was just about to ask for a cup of cocoa from the station café, when he heard a faint and weary flumping noise in the distance. Whatever it was, was having a ten-minute rest on every stair.

The sun, which had got tired of waiting, went off and the moon popped its face through the attic window just as the bear got its leg over the top stair and collapsed, exhausted, into one of Puff Puff's wagons.

"My goodness!" hooted Puff Puff, "What a sight he is! and to think I've waited all this time for him!" And he rattled back to the attic to show the other toys. But unfortunately, everyone had fallen asleep.

Prissy, the doll who was too good to be true, had gone to bed feeling cross because she had spent all day making welcoming fizzy drinks with ice-cream blobs, stuck with tiny paper umbrellas, and they'd all unfizzed and melted.

Penguin too had gone to a lot of bother.

He had made a special effort to brush his tummy smooth and find a new bow tie, and Moggy, who was not usually very generous, had kept a fish bone for the arrival of the newcomer. Now, they got up very early and made their way to the middle of the attic where a signpost said,

THIS WAY THAT WAY
THE OTHER WAY

The train shed was The Other Way, so that's where they went. There, outside the train shed, lay the bear, fast asleep on a pile of coal.

The toys stared at him in shocked silence. The bear had no fluff on him whatsoever. The inside of his ears were lined with cheap red felt, as were the soles of his feet, and there were holes in his head where moth grubs had been eating – probably mistaking him for dead. Also, the stuffing which had once been in his chest had wandered down to the lower parts of his body.

"What a disgusting animal!" gasped Prissy, disappointed because she had been hoping to marry him. Possibly.

Moggy quickly ate the bone he had been saving and thought what a narrow escape that had been – wasting a good fish bone on a character like THAT!

Penguin shuffled forward for a closer look. The bear was clutching a suitcase on which was a printed label. Penguin was cross-eyed, so he read it from back to front and side to middle. "It says, 'Sith si the ytreporp of EMOS TROS MAXFO ESQ' "

"No it doesn't!" scoffed Prissy. "It says, 'This is the property of Some Sort Oxfam Esquire.'"

There was also a single railway ticket, printed, "From Somewhere to the Attic."

"If only it had been a RETURN ticket," shuddered Prissy, covering her nose with a lacy handkerchief. "I would have much preferred that." She was just about to run home when the bear opened its eyes and stared at the three toys.

"Oh, I do apologise," he mumbled. "I must have fallen asleep before I had time to unpack my pyjamas.

"Pyjamas!" thought Prissy. "I bet he hasn't got any. I bet he wouldn't even know what they look like."

"Please allow me to introduce myself," the bear went on, "My name is Some Sort Oxfam Esq."

"Why Some Sort?" asked Moggy, who was a curious cat and liked asking questions.

11

"Because I am an orphan," explained Oxfam, "and so no one told me what KIND of bear I was. But I happened to hear someone one day calling me Some Sort."

"And why Oxfam?" asked Penguin.

"That is easier to answer," sighed the bear, "I came from a place called Oxfam, and have been travelling around ever since."

"In the back of a dustcart, I shouldn't wonder!" scoffed Prissy, tossing her yellow curls and going.

Oxfam watched her hurrying away and thought what a splendid woman she was. His heart fluttered inside his sawdust.

A little queue of attic toys came along. They were pretending that they were on a ramble, but they were really coming to have a look at the strange new bear.

They stood still and stared at Oxfam, open-mouthed. They noticed the cheap red felt lining in his ears and on the soles of

his feet, the stuffing from his chest which had moved further down his body, and the holes in his head where moth grubs had been eating. There was no fluff left on him at all, and some person, who must have been very bad at sewing, had tried to patch him up here and there.

"Hello," greeted Oxfam, badly wanting to be friends.

"Hello," said Tilly Losh, who was a rag doll and very cheeky. "We're just out rambling. We didn't mean to stop."

"Oh, I'd love to come with you," said Oxfam. "I'm used to rambling."

"Sorry," said Tilly Losh.

"I've got some walking boots in my case," said Oxfam. "I'll have them unpacked in a moment.

"And climbing ropes?" asked Tilly Losh.

"Er – no," said Oxfam.

"Then I'm terribly sorry, you can't come. The ground is rocky, and very squelchy in parts. Then there's Puddle Pond to cross. By the way, have you any swimming trunks in your suitcase?"

Oxfam shook his head.

"Or a snorkel perhaps?"

Oxfam shook his head again.

"Then I'm afraid it's absolutely impossible," decided Tilly Losh. "It would be far too dangerous. I dare hardly go myself."

When the bear looked disappointed, she added, "There are bandits hiding behind most of the rocks; squelch snakes in the mud, and I believe there's a big thingummy monster in Puddle Pond. There have been sightings." And off she rambled, whistling a careless sort of song.

As Oxfam could think of nothing better to do, and not having anywhere else to go anyway, he trudged round the attic in search of the library. There were many fine buildings. There was a corner shop, which

15

seemed to sell everything; a café, a castle, a magnificent Town Hall and a tall wooden building which looked rather like a huge bookcase and had "LIBREE" pinned on the front of it.

"Goodness," thought Oxfam. "Fancy a librarian not being able to spell 'library'!"

"Book, please," said the librarian.

"I haven't got one yet," said Oxfam.

"Huh! They all say that!" snapped the librarian. "If you knew the number of books which never come back. It's a SCANDAL!"

"I'm new here," mumbled Oxfam.

"Humph!" snorted the librarian, noticing at once the moth holes in Oxfam's head.

The library was full of ancient animals of one kind and another. Several seemed to be reading newspapers, but quite a few were sprawling about and looked fairly dead. In a far corner sat a gigantic gorilla. His hair

was dusty brown; his chest was shiny black leather. He had two small red eyes and was enormously affectionate, as Oxfam was soon to find out. His name was Boomer, and he was deeply engrossed in a book which was called, *The History, Past And Present, Of The Banana.*

At that moment, Prissy came teetering into the library. She always wore very high heels for she fancied they showed off her splendid legs. The fact that she often fell over was politely ignored by everyone.

The librarian rushed to serve her. "I'm looking for a book on lace-making," shrieked Prissy. "I have some very beautiful napkins. They were left to me

18

by my great aunt, who was the Duchess of Snoot, you know."

"I remember her well!" gushed the librarian.

"And I did think," went on Prissy, "that it would be rather lovely to edge them with some pretty lace. After all, one never knows WHO might drop in for dinner."

"One never does!" agreed the librarian, who had fish and chips for supper every night and had never had a visitor in the whole of her life.

She dashed off like a demented bee to find the book Prissy wanted. Whilst she was dashing, Prissy suddenly noticed the gorilla. "Boomer!" she cried, "What are you doing here?"

The gorilla leapt up and hugged Prissy until her face turned purple. "How lovely to see you!" Boomer grinned. "I was just reading this book about bananas," he explained.

"Delightful," said Prissy when she could

breathe again. "I too love history," she lied.

It was then she noticed Oxfam, who was standing gaping, and looking jealous. "Oh," said Prissy. "This is Oxfam, by the way. He has just arrived from Somewhere." She whispered in Boomer's ear, "I wouldn't bother with him too much. He's falling to pieces."

"Oxfam! My dear fellow!" boomed the gorilla. He looked around at the other animals in the library: the ones who were reading newspapers and those who were sprawled about looking fairly dead. "We could DO with someone new in the attic!" he added. And he hugged Oxfam so hard, little clouds of dust puffed out of him and floated round the library. Boomer handed his book in to be stamped.

"And where's YOURS?" snapped the librarian.

"I didn't choose one," apologised Oxfam.

"Didn't choose one!" the librarian

snorted. "They ALL say that – 'didn't choose one' – when half the time they have them stuffed up their jumpers and goodness knows where else. It's a SCANDAL, I tell you."

"Never mind her," laughed Boomer as they strolled across the attic towards the signpost. "I go This Way. Where do you go?"

"I go The Other Way," said Oxfam. And he trundled back to the train shed to his pile of coal and lay down.

It had been an exciting day. The moon was up again, and Oxfam lay there, thinking. The gorilla was going to be his friend, but, oh, how he wished the lovely Prissy would look upon him kindly.

• CHAPTER TWO •

A Home for Oxfam

THE NEXT DAY was so bright Mayor Bungle got out of bed early and put on his big golden chain. He was a clumsy-looking dog with a stomach several times too large for him. This was because he went to a different party nearly every day and always ate too much. He dragged his coach out of the garage and wheeled off in it, feeling enormously grand.

Mayor Bungle felt grand most days but

especially today because it was so sunny and his golden chain was shining more than usual. "I might even call another meeting," he thought as he rolled along. He liked calling meetings because everyone in the attic was forced to come, whether they wanted to or not, and he could sit on the platform in the Town Hall looking grander and grander as each minute ticked past. He was not always sure – and neither was anyone else – what the meetings were actually about, but that didn't matter too much. At least they were MEETINGS.

Sometimes the meetings were about DRAINAGE. Puddle Pond, for instance, which lay directly under the attic skylight, and overflowed whenever there was too much rain, was a problem. There was nowhere for the extra water to go. Perhaps water should be made to flow to the poorer part of the town where the less important people lived. The rabbits, for instance, could do with the extra water. With the number of children they had, they had washing days on Monday, Tuesday, Wednesday, Thursday, Friday, Saturday AND Sunday.

 Once Tilly Losh had thrown old cabbage stalks over into Prissy's garden and there had been a HUGE meeting about that, which everybody had enjoyed. There had been another meeting about there not being enough fresh fish in the attic. But the only one who had turned up for that

had been Moggy and so the meeting had to be cancelled. And lastly, Boomer had given a most interesting talk on banana-growing even though most people had left early.

As Mayor Bungle drove along, he looked with pride at all the lovely buildings. As there had always been plenty of building bricks lying around on the attic floor, most people had been able to build a home. The Town Hall of course was the most magnificent. It was built of blue, yellow and red bricks and was repainted every Tuesday. He INSISTED upon that. Of course, there were homes which were just holes in the skirting boards: homes of mice and spiders, but he didn't look too hard at those.

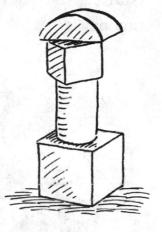

The mayor was just about to go home when he noticed the pile of coal outside the train shed and a lumpy-looking bear lying on top of it. A lumpier, more baldy, more moth-eaten animal the mayor had never seen in his life. A dustier, more badly stuffed, more pathetic animal he could not imagine.

"An old tramp!" he growled to himself.

"Good morning," said Oxfam.

"I thought it was till now," said Mayor Bungle. "Why are you lying on that pile of coal?"

"I don't know," said Oxfam. "I suppose it's because I have nowhere else to go."

"You mean you are HOMELESS!" gasped the mayor.

"Yes," said Oxfam. "I have been looking, but everywhere seems full up."

The mayor was delighted. He could have an absolutely enormous meeting about THIS. He dashed home at once and printed a notice. Mayor Bungle couldn't spell any better than the librarian, but he wrote,

NECKST MEATING
HOEMLUSSNUSS

EVREEBODY CUM. TONITE AT 7.30

SOSSIJ ROLES, CHOKLUT CAKE
AND LEMUNADE.
KNEWCUMMERS WELCUM?
ESPESHULLY BARES.

Everyone was very excited.

"It's to do with YOU, you know," Prissy told Oxfam as she dashed past his pile of

27

coal on the way to the hairdresser's. She could be seen nowhere important without her curls.

At 7.30 prompt, the Town Hall was full. The mayor was already sitting on his platform and next to him sat Oxfam, fastened to a chair with a rubber band because the mayor was anxious that he should not collapse before the meeting was over.

"Friends," Mayor Bungle began, "you all know why we are here, don't you?"

"Not really," squeaked a few of the mice.

Moggy gave them a nudge. He couldn't stand mice — unless of course they were tossed in butter and served with mushrooms and baked beans. He had to hold onto his whiskers to stop them trembling. It was a strict rule in the attic that no one ate anyone else.

"For the sake of those who are rather dim," continued the mayor, glancing at the mice, "this meeting is about homelessness. That is, people who have nowhere to live. Here we have a bear who is one such person. He is being forced to live on a pile of coal."

"Gosh!" said everyone.

"And how COLD that must be," the mayor went on.

"How terribly sad!" said Prissy.

"She's kind as well as beautiful," thought Oxfam.

"My first idea," the mayor was saying, "is that one of you could let this, er, dear old bear a room in your home. I would myself, but as you all know, I have to leave spare bedrooms for important visitors."

"That's my problem too!" gasped Prissy in a panic. "And I have so many parties."

"Of course, you do," agreed the mayor, who'd been to lots of them and didn't want some bald old bear cluttering up the place.

"I like a lot of water in my house," said Penguin. "It keeps my wings damp. My place would not be suitable for a bear who probably has aching bones already."

Moggy added, "I hardly have room for myself and I would be terrible company for such a lively-looking bear. I like to cat-nap most of the day, you see."

"I would just LOVE to have had Oxfam," Boomer excused, "but, as you all know, I have so many books in my place, I would have to get rid of most of my furniture."

"Idea number two will be after refreshments," announced the mayor. And everyone made a dash for the chocolate cake and sausage rolls. The meeting was nearly forgotten until the mayor reminded everyone that Oxfam was still homeless.

"We could build him a home of his own," squeaked the mice.

"Of course," said the mayor, pretending he hadn't heard," we could build him a home of his own."

"What a good idea!" agreed everyone.

"The mayor thinks of such clever things!" said Prissy.

Next day, everyone put on overalls and Wellington boots and tin hats. And they brought buckets and spades and rulers and screwdrivers and hammers and tubes of glue.

Boomer had a wheelbarrow full of building blocks which had been left over

from the Town Hall. "Do you want it south facing?" he asked Oxfam.

"Whatever," said Oxfam, happily.

It was lovely, thought the toys, to have something exciting to do. They decided to build the house halfway between the library and the train shed. That way Oxfam could either read a book or go off on a day trip.

"I would have loved him next door to me," declared Prissy, "but I'm afraid the noise from my dinner parties might disturb him."

"So thoughtful," agreed the mayor. He hoped one day to make the gorgeous lady his wife and he didn't want a moth-eaten old bear blundering around and possibly peering at him through Prissy's windows.

When the house was finished, it really did look very smart. Inside were a table and chairs, a cooker, a sink for washing dishes, a bed which Prissy had been trying to get rid of for some time and a little fireplace in which Boomer had painted some cosy red and yellow flames. Real fires were not encouraged as the mayor had said they were far too dangerous.

Everyone squashed into Oxfam's new house and wondered what they were going to get for tea. Oxfam wondered that too because he had never had visitors before. Especially so many, and they were all sitting there, politely, waiting to be fed.

"Excuse me one moment," he said. And he hurried off to the corner shop which sold everything. Mrs Bizzy was pouring different kinds of tea into little paper bags and arranging cakes and biscuits in the window.

"I've got people coming to tea," Oxfam told her.

"Ah!" said Mrs Bizzy, "then you'll be wanting cucumber sandwiches."

"I think so," said Oxfam.

"And eggy ones too?"

"Yes," said Oxfam.

"And perhaps your guests would like chocolate eclairs?"

"Yes," said Oxfam.

"And some iced fairy cakes," went on

Mrs Bizzy, delighted to have such a good customer.

"Yes," said Oxfam again.

"And I bet they'd LOVE some of my sticky doughnuts."

"I think they would," agreed Oxfam.

Mrs Bizzy packed everything into boxes

and told Oxfam to carry them carefully:
right way up.

"I will," said the bear.

Even Prissy had to admit that it was an
excellent tea-party.

"Well done, old fellow!" said Boomer.

And everyone went home – everyone,
that is, except the mice, who scampered
around the floor nibbling up the crumbs
until everywhere was spick and span.

"I think I'll wash the dishes in the
morning," yawned Oxfam, going happily
off to bed.

• CHAPTER THREE •

Oxfam's Birthday Present

NEXT DAY, the postman noticed there was a birthday card for Oxfam. He knew it was a birthday card because he was nosy and had unstuck the envelope. The postman always unstuck envelopes for he liked to read what was inside. He carried a little pot of glue in his bag so that he could stick them up again. Sometimes, big blobs of glue shot into somebody's letter and stuck all the pages together.

"That nosy postman has been at it again," Prissy was always saying.

Often, the mayor could only read half a letter, so was obliged to send half an answer. Like – "I'm sorry the road outside your house is... I shall... next week." Or, "Please make an appointment to come to the Town Hall on – "

The postman pushed Oxfam's card through the letter box and then cycled round the attic telling everyone that it was the old bear's birthday.

"I bet he's nearly a hundred years old," Moggy said.

"More like TWO hundred, I'd say," said Prissy.

"What are we going to buy him?" the mice wanted to know.

"Old people can't be bothered with presents," said Prissy. "They get past it." She wanted new curtains for her bedroom and didn't feel like wasting money on somebody else. "After all, we hardly know him."

"We could make him something," said
Boomer.

"Good idea!" squeaked the mice, but
they couldn't think what.

Nobody could think what.

"Come to think of it," said Boomer,
"there's a book in the library about making
things."

So everyone in the attic, except Oxfam, rushed to the library. "Books! Hey! Stop! Wait!!" screeched the librarian, as they all squashed past her.

Boomer found the right book. It was called, *A Hundred and One Easy Things to Make* and they all sat round it and looked at the pictures.

"It's got chocolate mice!" dribbled Moggy.

"It's got a stuffed cat," said one of the mice.

"Perhaps he'd like some roller skates," said Penguin.

"Huh! He'd fall off them!" scoffed Prissy.

They all looked under the table at Prissy's high-heeled shoes, but said nothing.

"I think we could knit him a little bow tie," suggested Prissy. "I have some old stockings I could unravel."

The toys thought that was the most boring idea they had ever heard.

"I think I've got it!" exclaimed Boomer, pointing a black hairy finger at a picture of a go-cart. "How about this?"

"Oh, it's super!" agreed everybody.

The go-cart in the book was bright red, had yellow wheels and a blue seat. Boomer took the book to the desk to be stamped.

The librarian looking suspiciously at the others, said, "And where're YOUR books?"

"We're all together," said Moggy.

"All together in a book-stealing gang, I bet!" snapped the librarian crossly.

They all went back to Boomer's house to see how they were going to make the go-cart.

"Instructions give me a headache," wailed Prissy.

"Well, you can put the kettle on," said Boomer. "This is a man's job, anyway."

"Huh!" said Prissy.

"I thought this book said a hundred and one EASY things to make," Penguin grumbled, after they'd been studying the instructions for a whole hour. "For one thing, where are we going to get a piece of board for the go-cart? That seems to be the most important bit."

"We could borrow a shelf from the library," suggested Moggy.

"We couldn't possibly do that!" gasped Boomer. "What time does the librarian go for her lunch?"

As it happened, the mice knew a back way into the library. They had spyholes everywhere and knew when the librarian put on her hat and went off for lunch.

"If we're only BORROWING the shelf," whispered Penguin, "why are we sneaking around like criminals?"

"And why are we wearing face masks?" squeaked the mice.

The gorilla, who was very wise, said, "It's better this way. You know how fussy the librarian is. She might say she only lends BOOKS – not shelves."

All the shelves were full up which meant moving a few of the books and hiding them in a cupboard.

We'd better hide the most boring books, then they won't be missed," Boomer decided.

"The arithmetic books," said Penguin.

"The gardening books," said the mice, who were house mice, not field mice.

"The history books!" shuddered Prissy.

"We'll hide the cookery books," decided Boomer.

And so they did. And the empty shelf was just the right size for a go-cart.

They scurried back to Boomer's house, feeling very pleased with themselves.

"Now we have to think how to make the wheels," Boomer said.

"Wheels are round flat things," said one of the mice.

"How clever you are!" scoffed Moggy.

Although they thought very hard, none of the toys could think how to make wheels. Prissy put the kettle on again, and the hot tea helped her to think. "When I used to live down in Somewhere," she began, "I can half remember there were some big round tins in a cupboard.

"What sort of tins?" asked Boomer.

"It said b-i-s-c-u-i-t-s on the lid," said Prissy.

"That spells biscuits," Boomer said.

"I know," lied Prissy.

"Four biscuit-tin lids would make excellent wheels," agreed Boomer, "but we wouldn't dare go down the Mountain Stairs to Somewhere. That's where the giants live. If they caught us, they'd throw us in the bin."

"We've got secret passages everywhere," boasted the mice. "We've got a back door into the biscuit-tin cupboard."

"Then you're the ones to go and get the lids," said Prissy.

"Oh, no!" trembled the mice. "We only said we knew where the biscuit-tin cupboard was. We didn't say we wanted to go there."

"Well, you don't expect ME to go down there, do you, in my best frock and my best shoes?" gasped Prissy. "And Boomer's too big and clumsy. And Penguin's cross-

eyed and would go in the wrong direction.
And Moggy would stray: all cats stray."

"Thank you," said Moggy, "I didn't want
to go anyway. I've been thrown in bins
before."

So the mice caught the two thirty train
to the end of the landing and then
disappeared through a hole in the skirting
board down to Somewhere and into the
biscuit-tin cupboard.

The four tins were still there. The mice
were shoving at the lids with their noses

and tugging at them with their claws, when they were disturbed by the sound of terrible footsteps. Two giants were thumping towards the cupboard.

"I want a biscuit, Mummy," said a small boy.

Terrified, the mice leapt into one of the tins and hid under some custard creams.

The mummy giant opened the cupboard door and shouted, "How many times have I told you to put the lids back on properly? The biscuits will go all soggy."

"I want a custard cream," said the enormous small boy.

"Oh, no!" squeaked the mice, trying to shrink themselves smaller.

"No, I don't," the small boy changed his mind. "I'll have a choccy one instead," and thumped off, munching loudly.

The mummy giant put the lids back on tightly, and slammed the cupboard door.

Then the mice had to struggle all over again, pushing with their noses and tugging with their claws. At last, they had all four lids, but found, to their distress, that they would not go through the mouse hole. Fortunately, mice are very good at nibbling holes through almost anything, but it took a very long time to nibble a hole big enough to squeeze the lids through. It was then easy to roll them along behind the skirting board.

"The daddy giant was watching the news. "What on earth's that noise behind the wall? he said.

"Hot water pipes I should think, darling, replied the mummy giant.

"Good heavens!" exclaimed the daddy giant. "It sounds more like a lot of tin lids being rolled along!"

"Tin lids!!!" laughed the mummy giant.

Puff Puff was waiting at the station at the top of the landing, and the tired mice climbed in. It was only one stop to the attic, but by the time they arrived, they were all fast asleep.

"Wake up, you lazy things!" said Prissy, prodding the sleepy mice. "You've been gone hours. How long does it take to collect a few lids?"

"Hours!" groaned the mice.

"I bet they've been lounging around eating biscuit crumbs and enjoying themselves," spat Moggy. "Mind you," he thought, "that would fatten them up." And he allowed himself a quick dream about mice tossed in butter and served with beans and mushrooms.

"If we don't hurry up," interrupted Boomer, "Oxfam's birthday will be over."

So everyone got to work. They

hammered and nailed and glued and painted.

Boomer had cut the legs off a small chair and nailed that on for the driving seat. Prissy had put a length of pink ribbon on the front of the cart with which to pull it. Moggy bit it off again and told her not to be such a silly woman. He found a piece of string instead.

"It looks magnificent!" agreed everyone when the job was finished, and they dragged it proudly to Oxfam's house and knocked on the door.

Oxfam opened the door and blinked in surprise.

"Happy birthday to you," sang the toys. "We've brought you a present."

"For ME!?" gasped Oxfam.

Prissy looked at the ceiling and thought what a slow-witted animal the old bear was. But Boomer said kindly, "Of course it's for you, dear fellow, and we hope you have many a happy ride on it."

51

Oxfam carefully sat down on the go-cart and everyone else squashed on behind him, and they whizzed round and round the attic until it was bedtime.

"It's the best birthday present I've ever had," thanked Oxfam.

CHAPTER FOUR

The Thingummy Monster

SOMETIMES, Prissy and Tilly Losh were best friends. Of course, Tilly Losh was only a raggy-looking doll and didn't know how to dress properly. Most days, she wore an old pinafore dress over a stripy jumper. The jumper looked as if it had once belonged to a bumblebee. A bumblebee who no longer wanted it back again. Prissy, on the other hand, was always extremely elegant.

But, Tilly Losh knew all the attic gossip and Prissy loved that. The pair of them would sit in the café for hours, eating scones and cream cakes and chatting. If there was a lot of gossip to tell, then they would have sausage and chips and a pot of tea each. If there WASN'T much to talk about, then Prissy might not even say hello to Tilly Losh. She wasn't, after all, a terribly important sort of doll.

Today, Prissy was in the mood for a good chat. She was anxious to know what Tilly thought of Oxfam. Maybe Tilly had found out things about him that would be interesting. Perhaps the old bear's parents had not been very grand, or he only had a bath on Saturday night, or he'd even been in prison.

She pulled on a pink hat and set off across the attic. She was very cross when Tilly didn't come to the door. "I bet the silly creature is still asleep," she thought. "Whenever does she get her dusting done?"

There is nothing more annoying in the whole world than going round to see someone who isn't in. Prissy peered through all the windows, and was just about to stick her nose through the letter box when one of the mice appeared.

"She's out," said the mouse.

"And how do you know that?" snapped Prissy.

"Because one or two of us popped in the other day to clean up her crumbs."

"You had no right to do that," Prissy scolded. "You are very nosy. Ah!" she

added, "Here comes the postman. Have you seen Tilly Losh lately?" she asked.

"Nope," said the postman. "She got a gas bill the other day and she hasn't been out to pay it. And she had another letter from Grandpa Losh saying he didn't feel too good – got a sniffle coming on, and she ain't answered that one either."

"And what ELSE have you read about other people's business?" snooted Prissy.

"Nothin' spectaclur. That be about it," answered the postman, not noticing at all that Prissy was being a bit nasty.

"Perhaps she's gone on a holiday," said Penguin, butting in. "She looks as if she could do with one."

"We could ALL do with one," said Prissy, "but we have duties. One can't just go tripping off when one FEELS like it."

If Tilly Losh had gone off on a lovely holiday without telling her, then Prissy would be very cross. "That doll only thinks about her own enjoyment," she said. "You should just see the dust on her dining table."

None of the toys could remember the last time they had seen Tilly, which was rather surprising as she was such a noisy doll.

"Ah!" said Oxfam, suddenly remembering, "she did come past my house the other day. She said something about rock climbing and squelch snakes. And, oh, yes, a thingummy monster in Puddle Pond."

"Oh, my goodness!" wailed Prissy. "We shall never see her again! My very best friend — squelched by snakes and squashed dead by a ferocious thingummy!"

"Eek!" said the mice.

"The girl's a fool!" said Moggy.

"We shall miss her dearly," Boomer sighed.

"There's a chance she might still be alive," added Penguin.

"How COULD she be!" snorted Prissy, who didn't want Penguin spoiling this new excitement, even though, of course, it was terribly sad.

"I shall go and look for her," said Oxfam.

The toys looked at him in amazement: an old bear like him, willing to risk his life for a girl he hardly knew.

"Oh no, dear fellow, we couldn't let you," said Boomer.

"Yes, we could," squeaked Prissy. "It was his idea. He would be disappointed if we didn't let him go."

I'll take the go-cart," said Oxfam, "then if Tilly is not feeling well she can lie down on it."

A faint, very faint, feeling of admiration

stole over Prissy. "I'll lend you a blanket," she said. "My very best friend might be glad of it."

Moggy had headache pills and sticking plasters. Penguin and Boomer went to Mrs Bizzy's shop and bought teabags, packets of crisps and some jelly babies.

By the time the go-cart was packed, there wasn't an enormous lot of room left for Oxfam himself, but he reckoned that after Tilly Losh had eaten all the jelly babies, there would be.

"Goodbye!" waved the toys. "Good luck! Watch out for the squelch snakes!"

Bravely, Oxfam trudged off across the attic and was soon out of sight.

"You're CRYING!" sniggered Moggy.

"No, I'm not," sniffled Prissy. "It's that cloud of dust which just pouffed out of Tilly's letter box."

Oxfam felt he'd been walking for many hours when he came in sight of some very big rocks. They were piled high like parcels in a post office on Bank Holiday.

"Oh dear!" he thought, "Now I know why Tilly Losh wouldn't let me go with her."

Younger bears, of course, are very good at climbing. They can climb almost anything. Their claws can stick into tree trunks and hang onto slippery stones. But Oxfam was not young any more. He would climb up one rock and then slither down two.

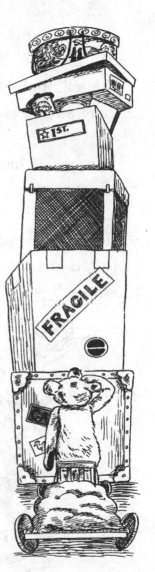

"I think I must have discovered Everest," he puffed. "Any higher and my head might bump into the sun."

But somewhere around teatime, he reached the top

61

and sat down. Sadly, he noticed that all the teabags and the packets of crisps had dropped off the back of the go-cart, but the jelly babies were still there because they were sticky. He ate a few and felt better.

Far below him stretched Puddle Pond. As he got nearer, he could see that where the edge of the pond had turned the floorboards soft and slimy, there lay a great mass of heaving squelch snakes. The squelch

snakes were wriggly and rubbery and looked as if they might have escaped from some joke shop.

The parent snakes must have had lots of children, and those children had grown up and had children of their own until now there must have been about five hundred of them, or more. They were all painted bright yellow and were not nice. They weren't even nice to each other. They slithered around on top of one another and didn't care whether those underneath could breathe or not. The words "excuse me", or "I'm sorry" were quite unknown to them. All they thought about all day was what they were going to eat, or WHO. Hardly anybody ever walked past them because they knew what would happen to them if they did. Often, the squelchers wished that a big fat animal would come along and then they could have a feast. But none did.

But suddenly there WAS an animal coming towards them. He wasn't fat, but he was pretty big. He didn't look exactly tasty, but the squelch snakes were so hungry that didn't worry them. They began to push each other and slide towards the edge of the pond. Then all five hundred of them stood up on their tails and hissed, and their horrible little forked tongues shot in and out of their mouths.

Oxfam was very worried. He couldn't go back, and he couldn't walk over the snakes. There was a small path round the side of the pond, but the squelch snakes could still easily reach him. Perhaps they would get tired of standing on their tails. But they didn't. They swayed backwards and forwards all together, staring at him and waiting. Perhaps they had already eaten poor Tilly Losh, yet there was no sign of anything belonging to her – like a hair ribbon or the left-overs of a shoe.

Oxfam sat down on his go-cart and wondered what to do. Then he spotted the jelly babies. They were shining in the sunshine and looked very juicy. Surely everybody loved jelly babies – even squelch snakes. Maybe the jelly babies could save his life. He picked them up and threw them as far as he could into the water. The snakes leapt on them joyfully and fought with each other greedily. Oxfam rushed along the little path, and before the squelch snakes had realised that the bear would have made a much better meal, he was far away.

"What a terrible thing to happen! or nearly happen," he puffed. And maybe it had already happened to poor Tilly Losh. He must walk on to the other side of Puddle Pond. If she had been lucky enough to escape the squelchers, there was still the thingummy monster to rescue her from. No doubt it was enormous, and it was bound to be fierce. He had never met a monster but he'd seen lots of pictures of them and none of them had looked awfully pleasant. He wished he had brought some lemonade. Now all he could think about was lemonade.

*   *   *

Puddle Pond lay immediately under the skylight. The skylight leaked, so when it rained outside, Puddle Pond was quite full, and if it didn't, it wasn't. Today it wasn't. But rain or no rain, Puddle Pond was always quite deep. In the middle of it was one building block, to which Tilly Losh was clinging – and screaming. She was screaming because the thingummy monster was whizzing round and round her in big circles. The thingummy was massive. It was bright green with red spikes down its back and had a long neck
and a tiny
head.

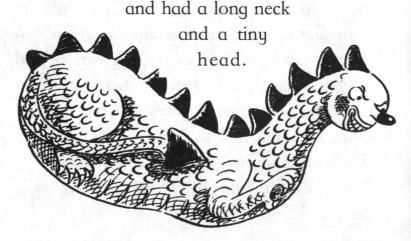

It seemed to be hugely enjoying frightening Tilly. Oxfam was aghast. This monster looked far more terrible than the squelch snakes. But Tilly's screams melted Oxfam's heart and he plunged into Puddle Pond.

The thingummy monster saw him coming and zoomed towards him. "Hee hee! More fun!" it thought.

Oxfam struck out with one sharp claw. Then the most amazing thing happened – air started to hiss out of the thingummy's tummy and as it did so, the animal began to whizz all over the place like a mad thing until it lay, still and flat, on the water, like a piece of rubber.

"Oh, no! How mean of you," it groaned. "You've gone and popped me. I was only having a bit of fun."

Oxfam and Tilly Losh felt awful.

"I didn't know you were just pretending," Tilly began to cry a bit, "but I think you can be mended." And she laid him carefully on the go-cart.

Meanwhile, the furious squelch snakes knew that Tilly Losh and the old bear would have to come back past them. This time, they weren't going to be fooled by the old jelly baby trick. Once again they stood up on their tails and waited, swaying this way and that.

Oxfam and Tilly Losh were not looking forward to seeing them, but when the squelch snakes saw the thingummy monster

lying, as they thought, stone dead on the back of the go-cart, they were shocked. Anyone who could do battle with the terrible thingummy and squash it flat must be very fierce indeed, and they dived for the water's edge and slithered away in a panic.

"Fancy that!" exclaimed Oxfam as they strolled easily along the side path.

"What big babies they are!" laughed Tilly Losh.

At the bottom of the rocks, they found the packets of crisps and stopped for a small picnic.

The toys were extremely excited when they saw Oxfam pulling Tilly along in the go-cart.

"My dear friend!" cried Prissy, hugging and kissing Tilly Losh in an absolute rapture. Then she forced herself to give Oxfam a little peck on the cheek and muttered, "So brave!"

Then she noticed the thingummy lying

on the go-cart. "What on earth is that?" she shuddered.

"It's the thingummy monster," explained Tilly. We were hoping someone could make him better."

"Do we want to?" asked Prissy.

"Yes, he's very nice really," Tilly said.

"He's got a small hole in his tummy," Penguin noticed.

"Just a little mistake," mumbled Oxfam.

Penguin fetched some sticking plaster and covered the hole. Then they all took turns puffing the air back into the monster until he was his old jolly self again.

"He can live in my washing-up bowl," cheered Tilly Losh," and I can lift him out when I wash my dishes."

"And that won't be very often," said Prissy.

Margaret Stuart Barry lives in Richmond in Yorkshire, and had a wonderful time writing about the Attic Toys, who are all based on her favourite friends from childhood! Of course more toys are always pushing into her memory, wanting to be included – so watch out for more stories!

Tessa Richardson-Jones drew the pictures, and now has all the toys living on her desk!

Watch out for more ATTIC TOYS ADVENTURES

The Attic Toys

MOGGY
THE WITCH'S CAT

FREE STAND-UP TOY

MARGARET STUART BARRY

PICTURES BY TESSA RICHARDSON-JONES

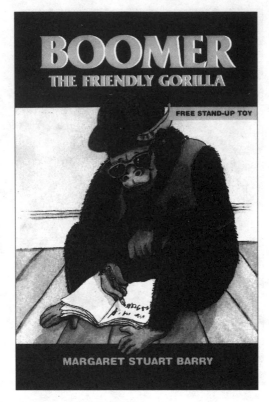

The Attic Toys

TILLY LOSH
THE RAG DOLL

FREE STAND-UP TOY

MARGARET STUART BARRY
PICTURES BY TESSA RICHARDSON-JONES